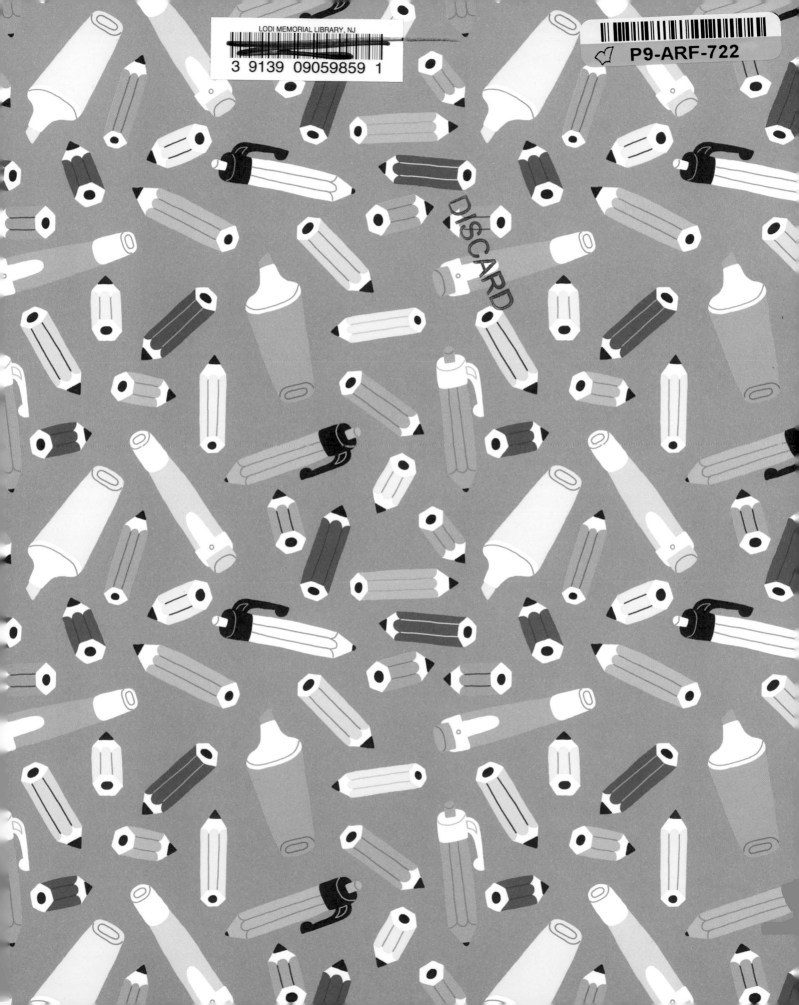

Penpals Forever

Written by C K Smouha
Illustrated by Jürg Lindenberger

British Library Cataloguing-in-Publication Data.

A CIP record for this book is available
from the British Library.
ISBN: 978-1-908714-71-8
First published in 2020

Cicada Books Ltd
48 Burghley Road
London, NW5 1UE
www.cicadabooks.co.uk

Printed in Poland

PENPALS

Forever

...when a huge, white **thing** came diving
out of the sky towards them.

Upon close
examination it appeared to
be a gigantic letter.

What a coincidence,
thought Freddy.
I am grey and I have big
ears and a big nose,
and I am also eight years old!
I will write back immediately.

Annabel was
busy in her lab when the
doorbell rang.

Thanks!

The postman
handed her a letter the size
of a watermelon seed.

Annabel peered closely,
but the words were too small
for her to read.

She put on her
glasses, but she still
couldn't read it.

She got her
magnifying glass, but even
that didn't work.

Finally, she went into her laboratory and,
using tweezers, carefully put the teensy letter
under the microscope. It said:

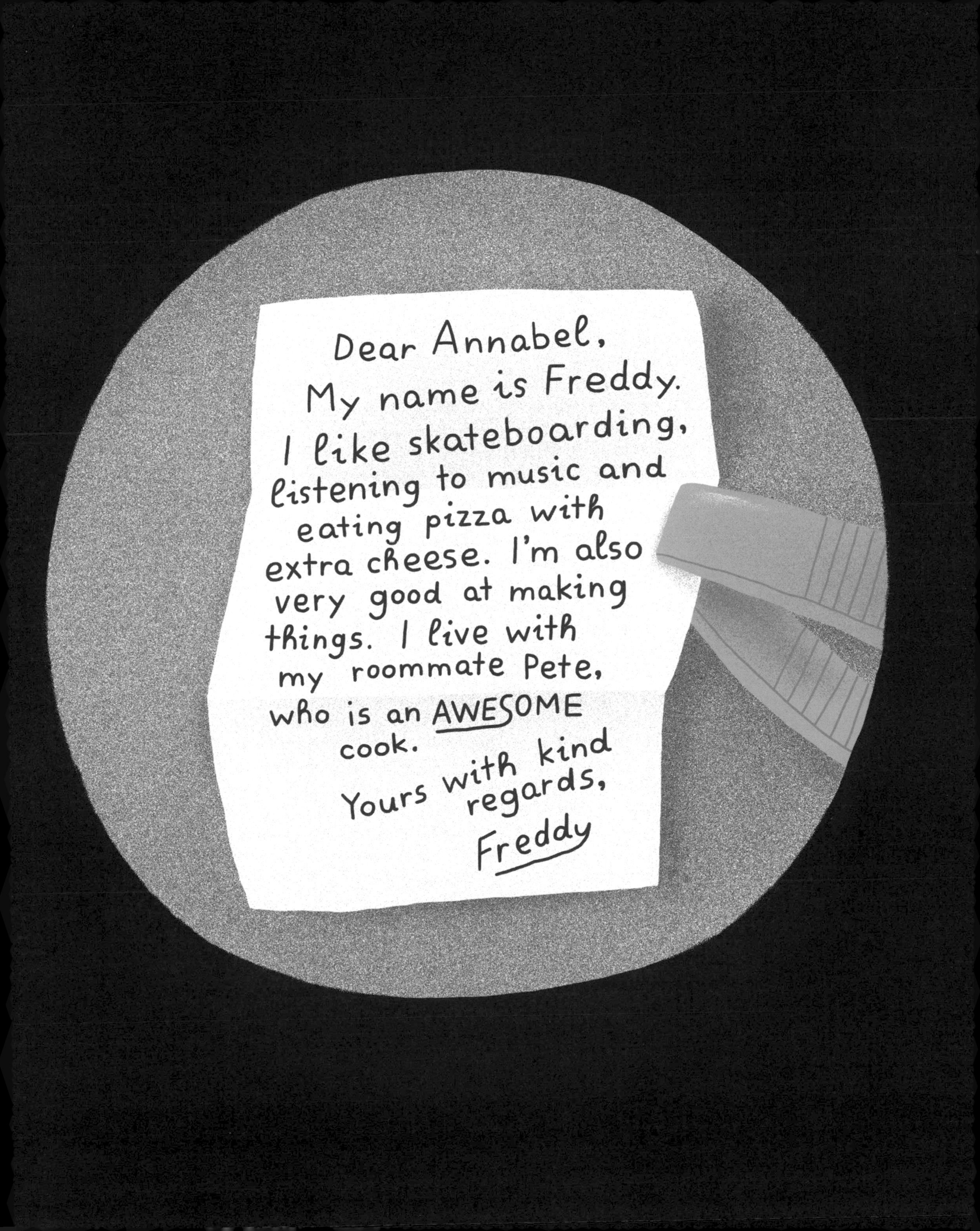

Dear Annabel,

My name is Freddy. I like skateboarding, listening to music and eating pizza with extra cheese. I'm also very good at making things. I live with my roommate Pete, who is an AWESOME cook.

Yours with kind regards,

Freddy

Annabel and Freddy
wrote back and forth
each week.

Dear Freddy,
I went for a hike
today and stubbed
my toe on a big rock.
I looked closely
and found it was
a termite mound.
It was hard as
concrete and
nearly two
feet tall!

Yours faithfully,
Annabel

Dear Annabel,
Today Pete and I went to see our favourite band, Radical Rodents, it was AWESOME! We had to take the long way home so we wouldn't bump into nasty Cheddar Dave and his gang, but it was worth it. I have made myself a brand new skateboard. Here's a picture!
Your pal,
Freddy

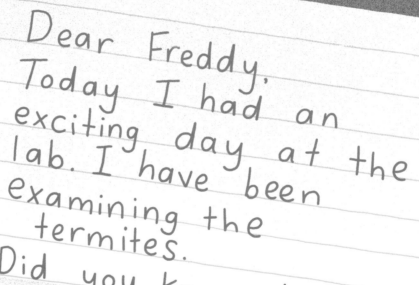

Dear Freddy,
Today I had an exciting day at the lab. I have been examining the termites.
Did you know they never sleep? They work 24 hours a day... Fascinating creatures

Love,
Annabel

Dear Annabel,
Today I almost managed to do a kickflip tailgrab on my skateboard, but halfway through, Cheddar Dave snatched my board away and I fell flat on my back. Pete made me pizza for dinner so that made me feel better.

Yours.
Freddy

Dear Freddy,
Cheddar Dave sounds like a real meany. The termite mound in my garden is nearly four feet tall.

I hope you're keeping safe. Write me back soon. Please!

Kindly yours,

Annabel

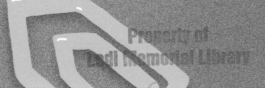

Dear Annabel,
Things have been getting a bit tricky with the Cheddar Gang. I wish they would just leave us alone. We haven't gone to the skatepark for a week.
Any advice for your buddy?

Freddy

And then one day, Freddy's letters stopped coming.
One week passed. Then two. Then three. Annabel was getting worried.

Finally, Annabel could bear it no longer.
She packed her bags and set off to find her friend.

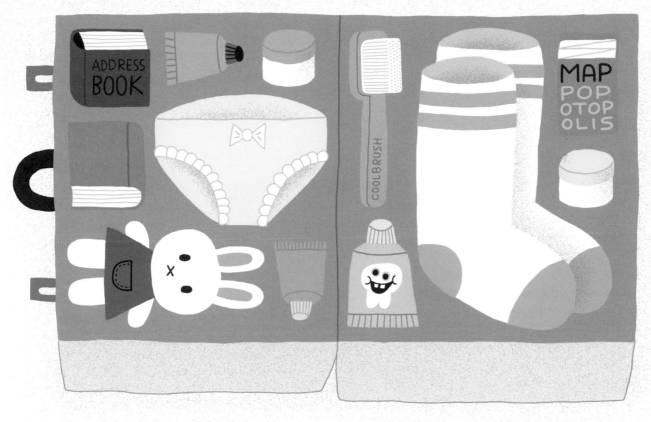

The city was big.

But so was Annabel.

She marched straight to Freddy's house.

But Freddy was nowhere to be seen.

And in his place was a gang of shady looking characters.

WHO ARE YOU AND WHERE'S FREDDY ???

But where could he be?

She wandered here
and there.

678

Until she caught a whiff
of something delicious.
Could it be... **pizza**?

She let her big nose lead the way...

Using her huge trunk, Annabel hoovered up nasty Cheddar Dave and his friends.

And then they took Annabel to all their favourite places.

It was brilliant.

But after a while, Annabel started to feel homesick.

I've had a great time, but I miss my home.

Oh please don't go!

My termites will be missing me. But why don't you come with me?

Okay!

So Freddy and Pete packed their bags and joined her.

Are you sure you'll need a hard hat?

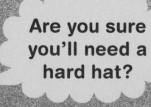

CHEESE SNACK

SO LO

YOGA
MARG RET B

You can never be too safe.

Just then,
a wonderful smell
drifted over
the savannah.

Annabel and Freddy
lifted their big grey noses
and followed it.

After that, the three friends had a wonderful time hiking...

…and exploring…

…and making
exciting discoveries.

It had been an exciting few weeks, but Freddy and Pete were happy to get back to their cosy mousehole.
Things went back to normal, and they never had any more trouble from Cheddar Dave and his gang.

They skated...

...and cooked...

...and made things.

But the thing they most looked forward to...

Freddy
Mousehole 438
Popotopolis
U.K.

...was the post.

The End